POP!

Written by
Jason Carter Eaton

illustrated by
Matt Rockefeller

:01
First Second
New York

It was a beautiful day and Dewey was all alone blowing bubbles.
You don't need a friend to blow bubbles.

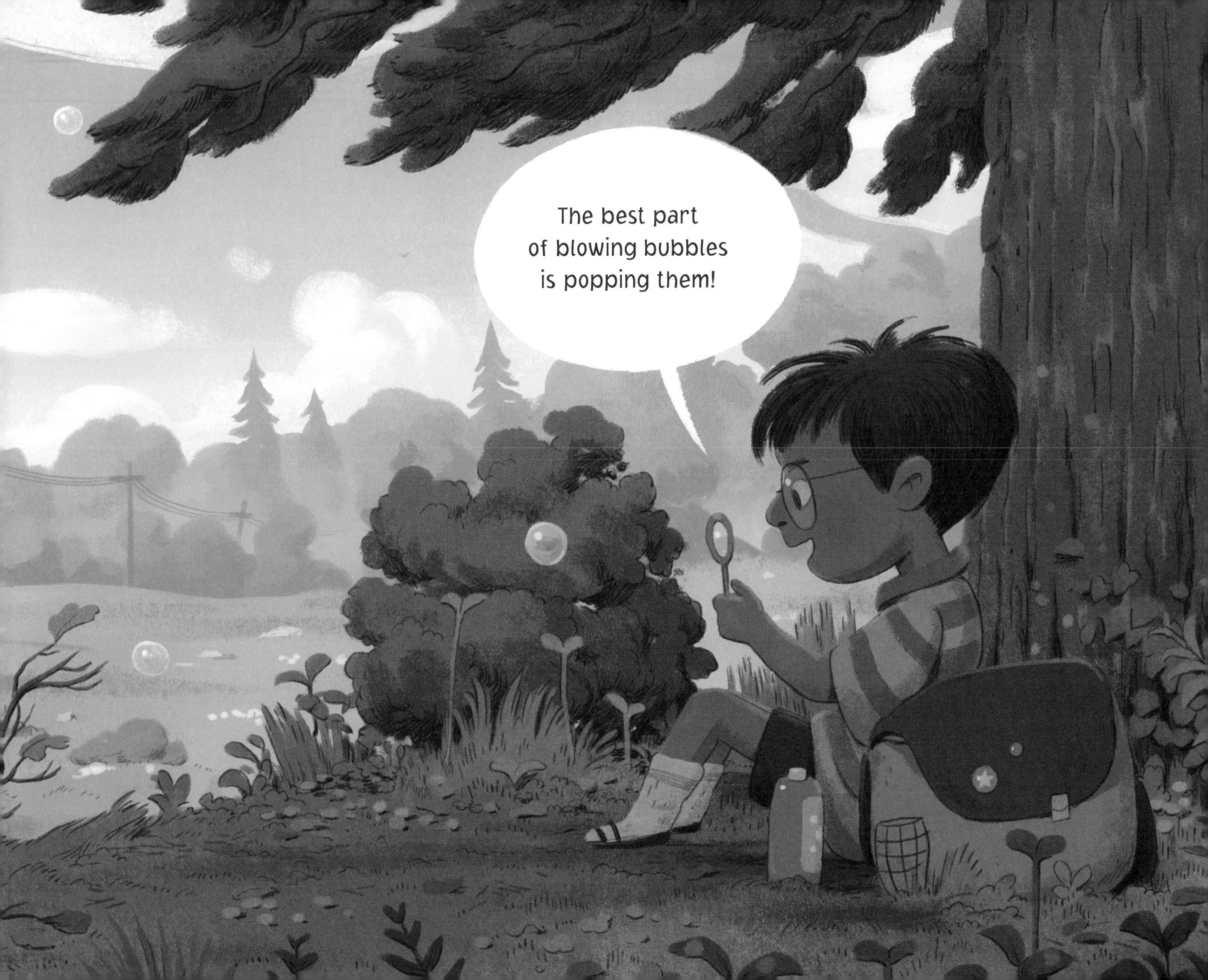
The best part
of blowing bubbles
is popping them!

But no sooner had he said that . . .

than he just missed popping . . .

. . . the very last one.

It caught a slight breeze and he stood up so he could see where it was going.

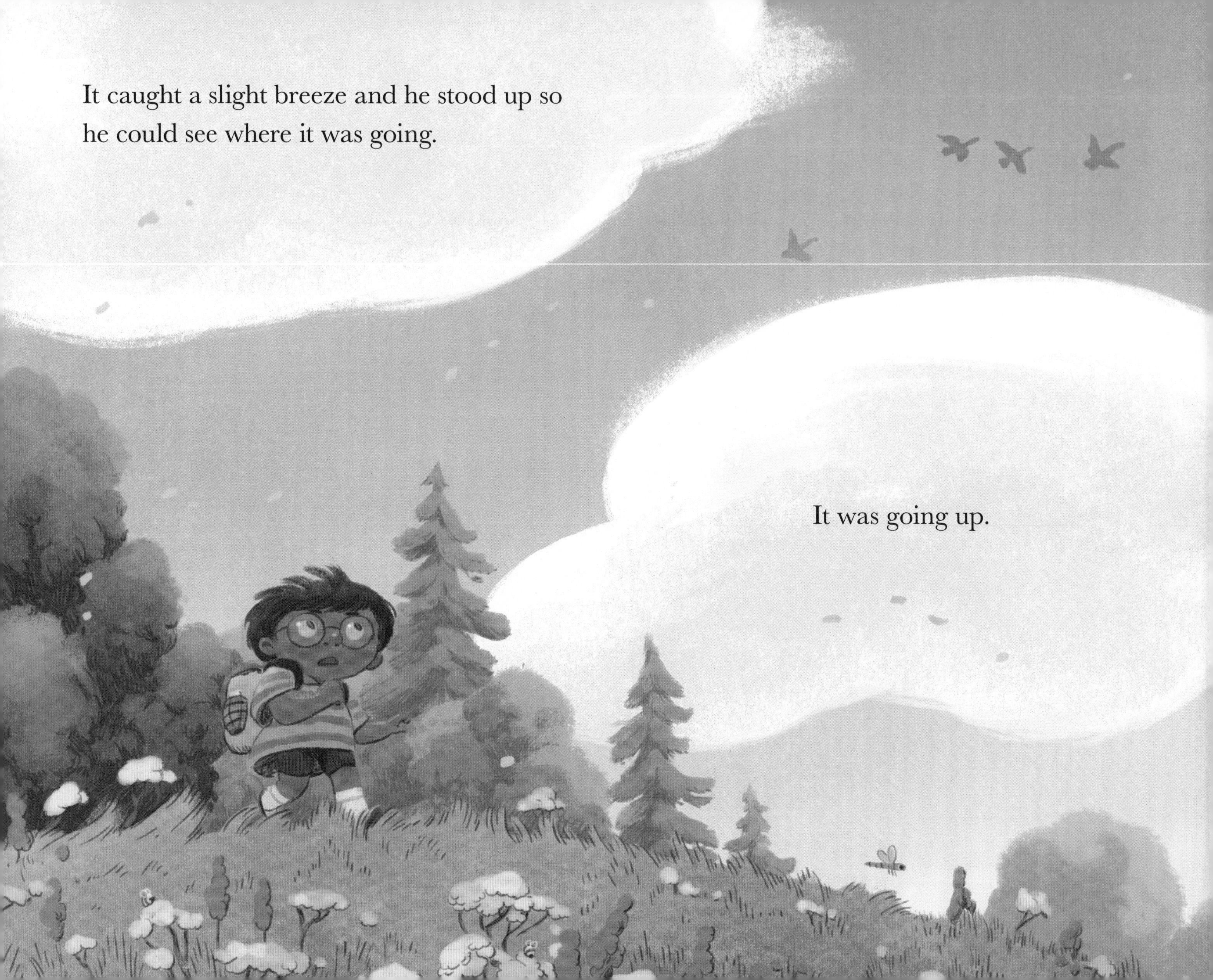

It was going up.

So Dewey jumped up and down to try to reach it. But in almost no time at all it was out of reach again.

He'd need to jump higher.

The backyard trampoline would do the trick.

Almost. This was one elusive bubble.

Thinking quickly, he climbed up on top of his jungle gym.

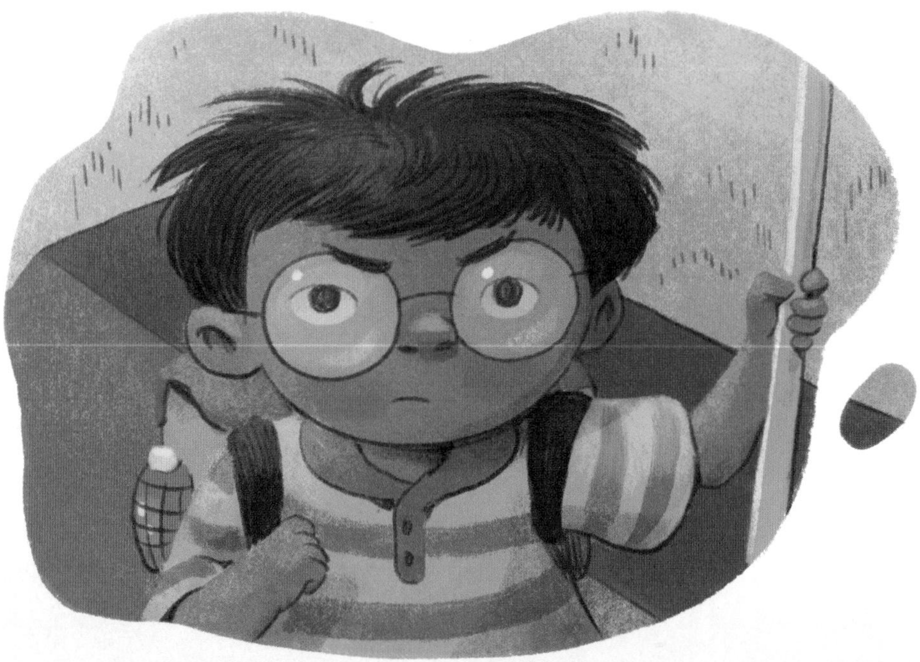

And watched as the bubble sailed right over him.

This was going to be harder than he thought. Dewey quickly fetched a ladder and raced to the roof of his house. But the bubble was way, way past that already.

He grabbed his telescope.

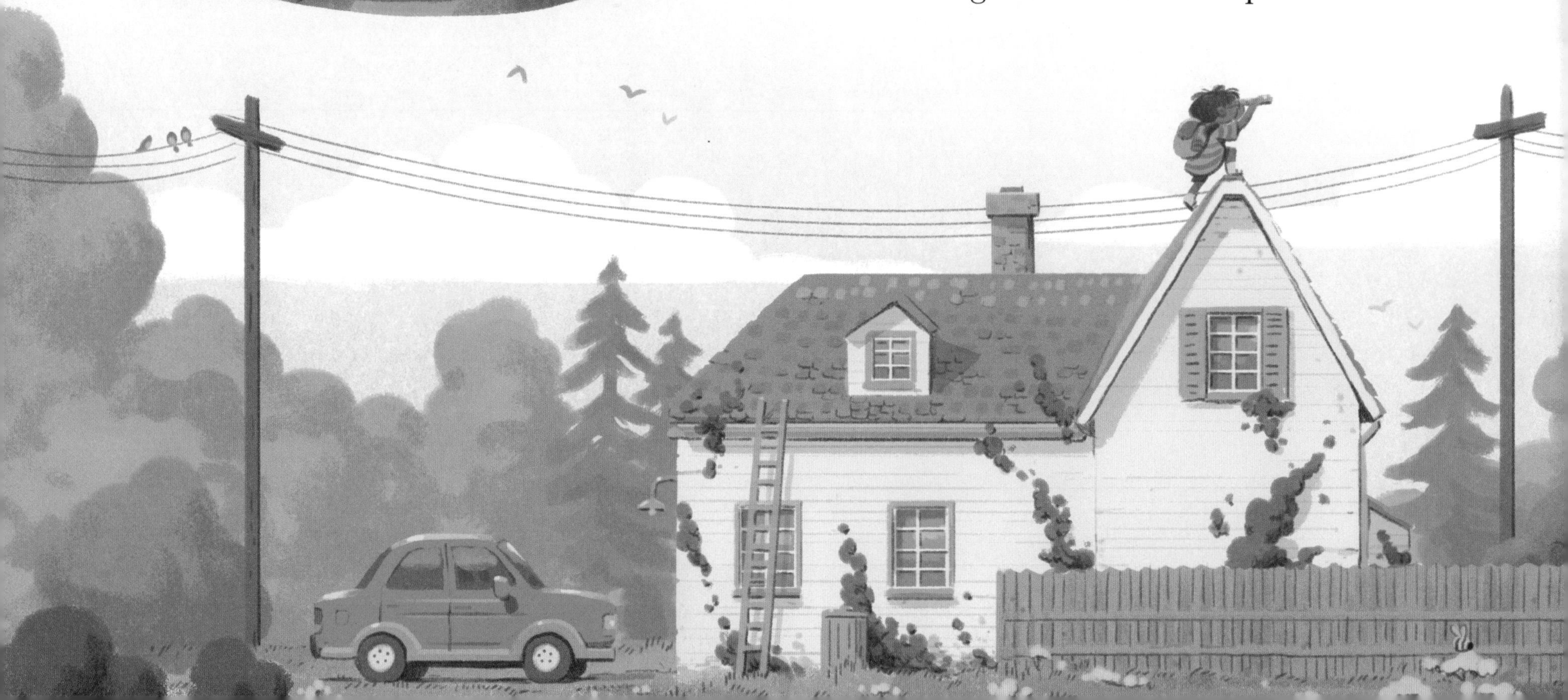

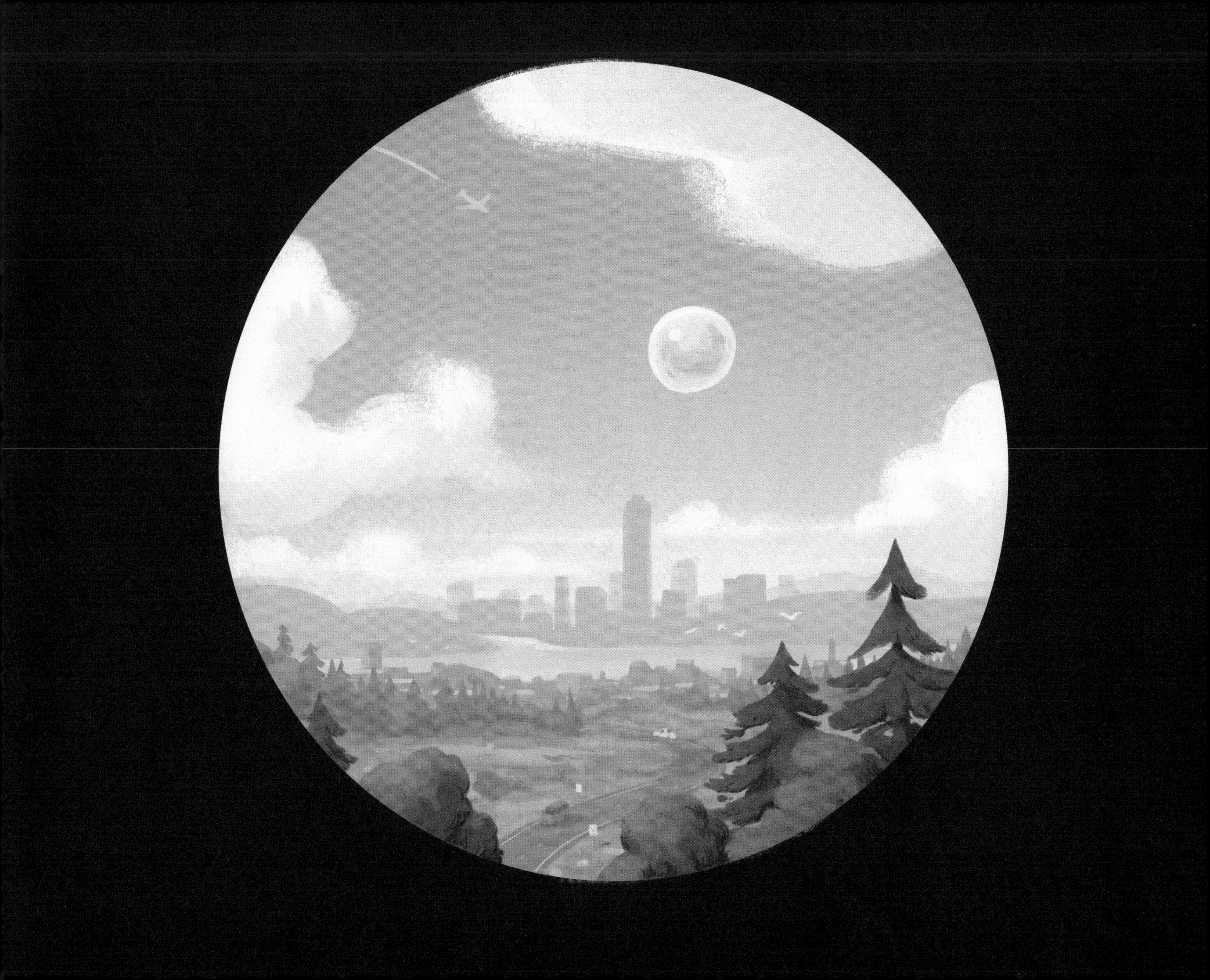

There was a really tall building in town.
Dewey hopped on his bike and rode like the wind.

When he reached the building he dove into the elevator and pressed
the button, emerging moments later on the top floor . . .

. . . just moments after the bubble.
He'd need to get higher still.

Just then a man with a hot air balloon passed by. Dewey quickly explained the situation.

And of course the man wasted no time giving Dewey his balloon. After thanking him, Dewey was off.

He quickly gained on the bubble, but there must have been a crosswind, because soon they were on opposite ends of the sky.

"Closer," thought Dewey.
"I have to get closer."

The helicopter flying past would do nicely.
And after some explaining and thanking, it was all his.

The problem with helicopters, however, is that they can only go so high. And this bubble was showing no signs of slowing down. He'd definitely need something with more *oomph* . . .

. . . like that biplane, which took some
serious explaining and thanking
but was totally worth it.

Up, up, up went the bubble, with Dewey and his biplane quickly closing the gap. Though not quick enough for his taste.

His taste was more suited to that F-16 fighter jet on the horizon.

Of course, it took a ton of explaining and thanking, but in the end Dewey knew it would pay off.

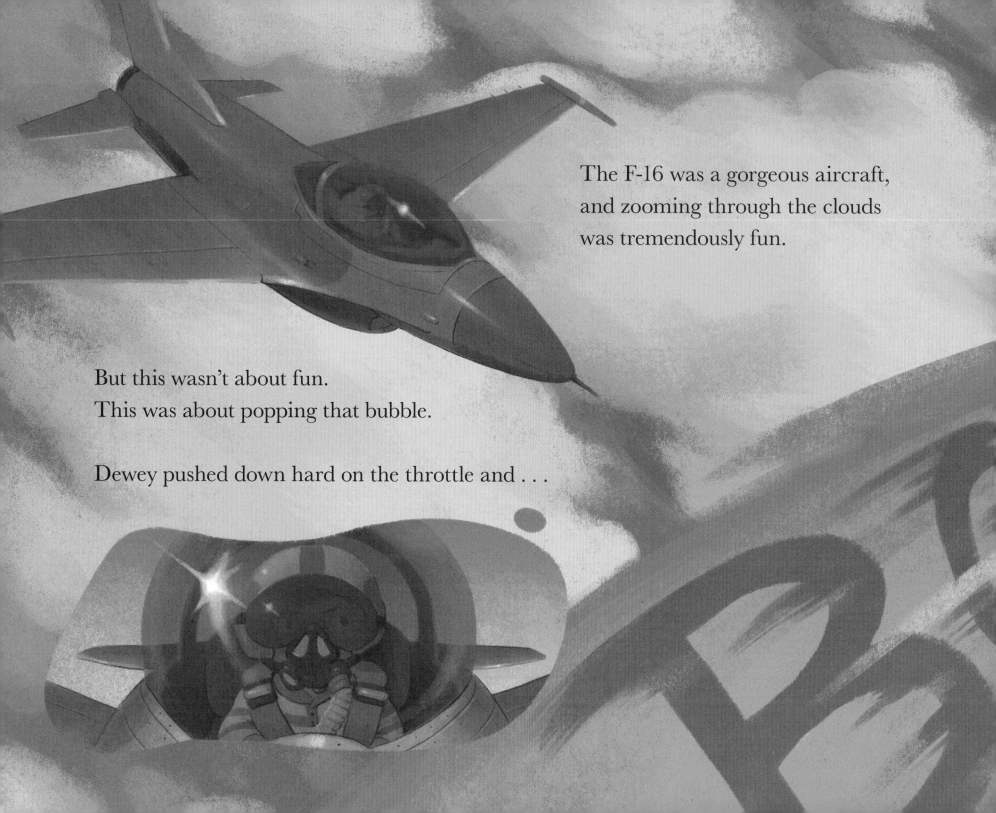

The F-16 was a gorgeous aircraft,
and zooming through the clouds
was tremendously fun.

But this wasn't about fun.
This was about popping that bubble.

Dewey pushed down hard on the throttle and . . .

. . . soared upward toward the bubble.
He knew F-16s could only go up to
50,000 feet, so he'd need to catch it
before then.

It was close . . .

. . . but not close enough.

He'd never be able to catch it now.

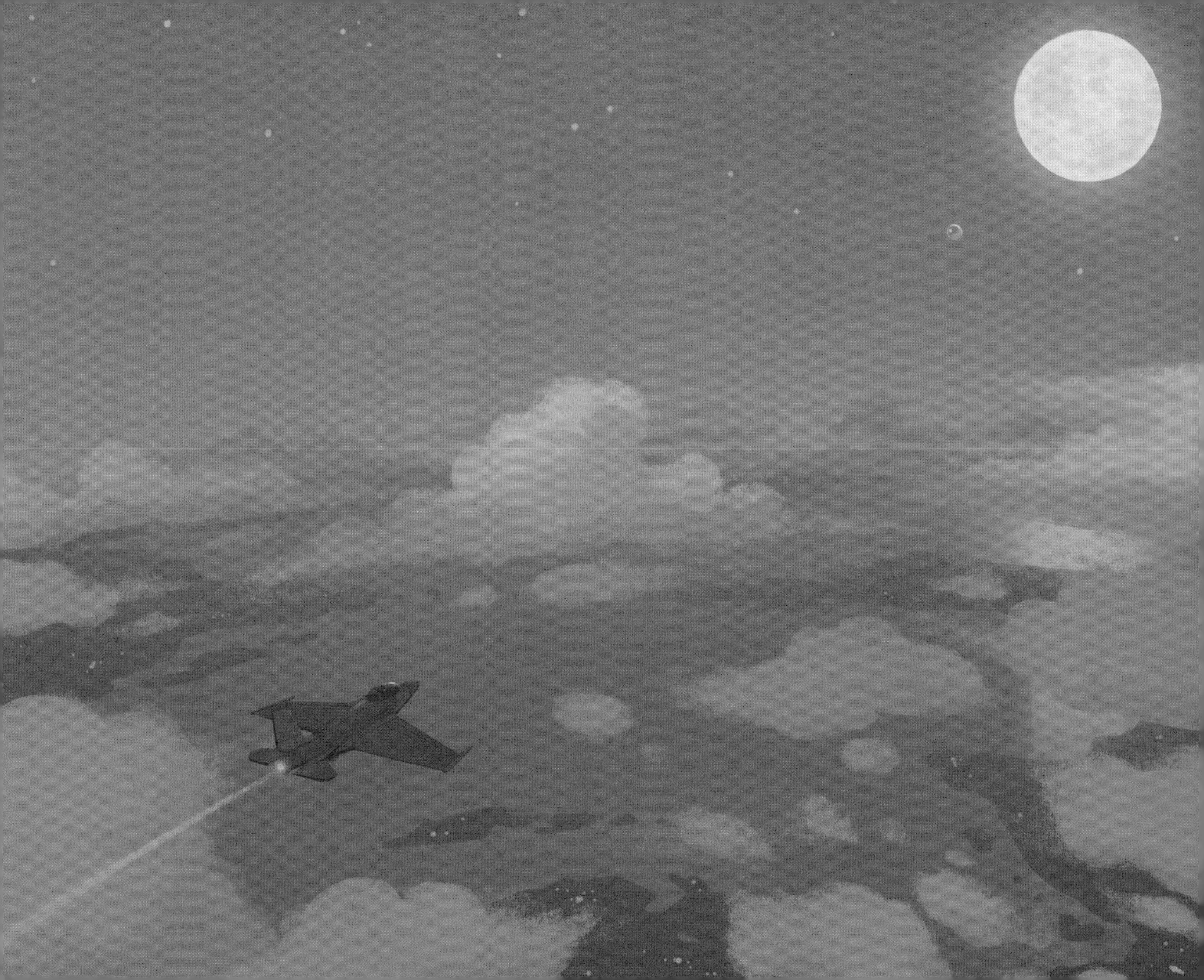

Not unless it just happened to be the day of the moon launch.

Which it did. Though as Dewey did his explaining and thanking,
he knew this was probably his last chance to catch that bubble.

But none of that mattered now.
He was in the fastest, most powerful
rocket in the world.

There was no stopping him!

Except for the fact that the rocket stopped on the moon.

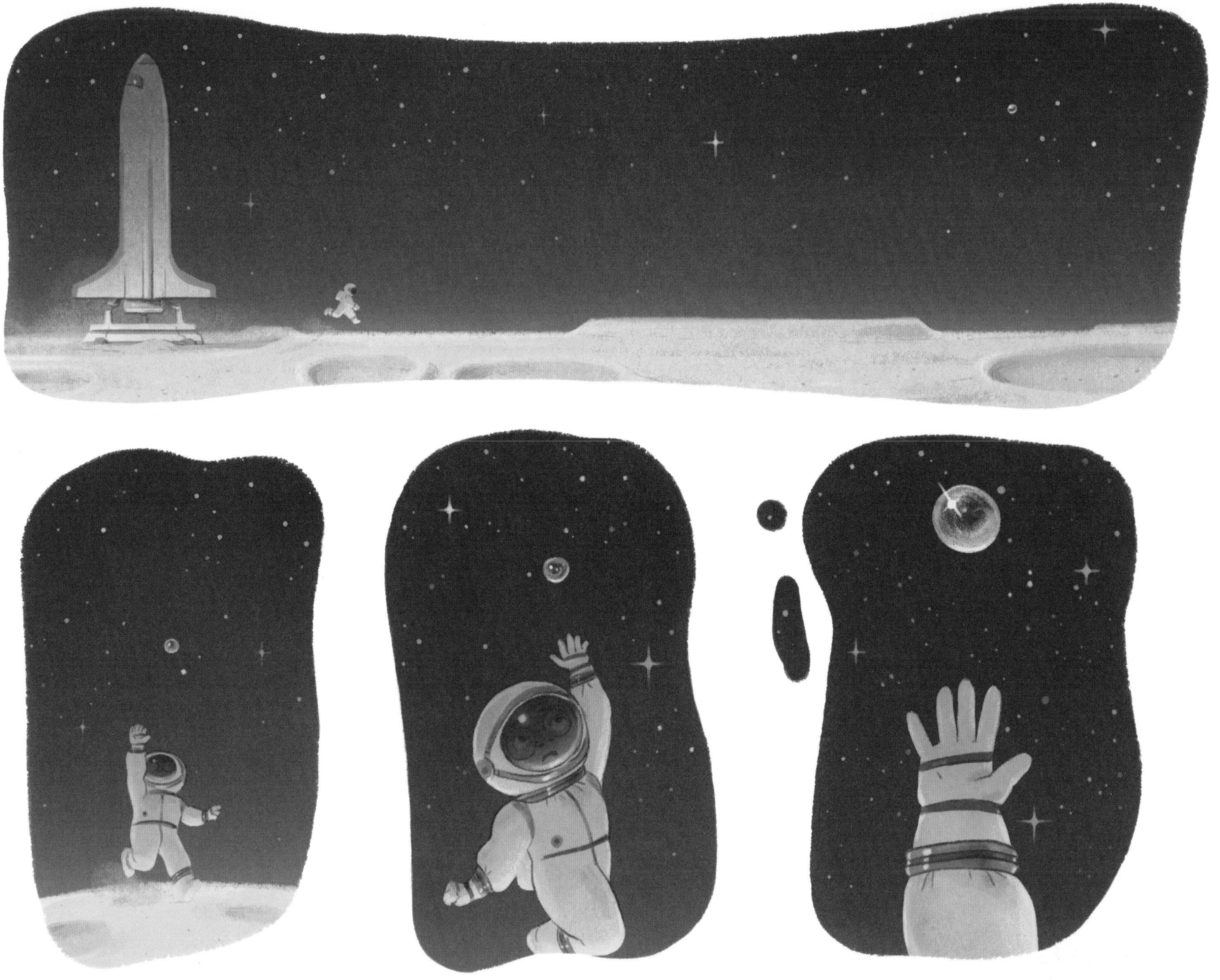

Dewey returned home. He was sad that after all that effort he'd never pop the bubble.

That night, just before bed, he pulled out his telescope to see if he could spot his bubble.

But something was blocking his view.
A bubble. But not his.

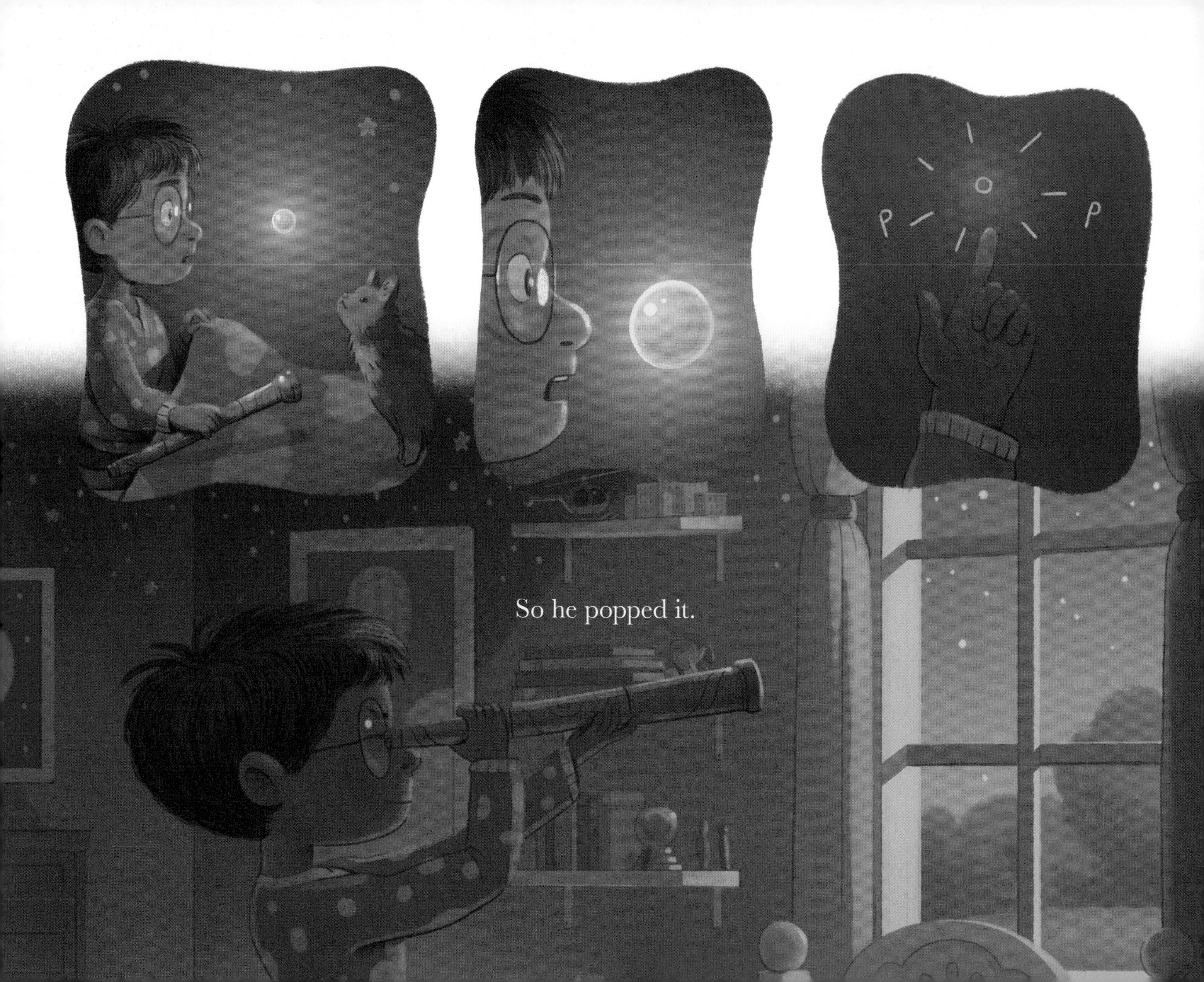
POP

So he popped it.

Now Dewey could see where that bubble had come from.
And where *his* bubble had gone.

And he knew
he'd found a friend.

First Second

Published by First Second
First Second is an imprint of Roaring Brook Press, a division of Holtzbrinck Publishing Holdings Limited Partnership
175 Fifth Avenue, New York, NY 10010

Library of Congress Control Number: 2017909422

ISBN: 978-1-62672-503-4

Our books may be purchased in bulk for promotional, educational, or business use.
Please contact your local bookseller or the Macmillan Corporate and Premium Sales Department
at (800) 221-7945 ext. 5442 or by e-mail at MacmillanSpecialMarkets@macmillan.com.

First edition, 2018

Book design by Matt Rockefeller and Andrew Arnold
Printed in China by Toppan Leefung Printing Ltd., Dongguan City, Guangdong Province
1 3 5 7 9 10 8 6 4 2

Drawn and painted digitally with custom brushes in Photoshop.